THE GREATEST ADVENTURES IN THE WORLD

Beowulf
THE HERO

TONY BRADMAN & TONY ROSS

ORCHARD

D1497687

ORCHARD BOOKS

The text was first published in Great Britain in a gift collection called
The Orchard Book of Heroes and Villains with full colour illustrations by Tony Ross, in 2008
This edition first published in hardback in 2010
First paperback publication in 2011

3 5 7 9 10 8 6 4 2
Text © Tony Bradman 2008
Illustrations © Tony Ross 2010

A CIP catalogue record for this book is available from the British Library.

ISBN 978 1 40830 574 4

Printed and bound in Germany by GGP Media GmbH, Poessneck

The paper and board used in this book are made from wood from responsible sources

Orchard Books
An imprint of Hachette Children's Group
Part of The Watts Publishing Group Limited
Carmelite House, 50 Victoria Embankment, London EC4Y 0DZ

An Hachette UK Company
www.hachette.co.uk
www.hachettechildrens.co.uk

CONTENTS

CHAPTER ONE

WARRIOR

L ONG AGO, IN THE FAR-OFF days of legend, when being a hero still counted for something in the cold, hard lands of the north, a young warrior called Beowulf heard a tale that set his mind racing with dreams of glory.

One night, a monster called Grendel had crept into the hall of a Danish chieftain by the name of Rothgar. The monster killed many of Rothgar's warriors, and left nothing but their blood splattered on the walls. Grendel had returned the next night, and every night since.

So Rothgar had to leave his hall empty in the sunless hours, and his people lived in terror.

It was said that no one could stand up to Grendel and survive, although many mighty warriors had tried their hands against him. That made it even more tempting for Beowulf to take on the challenge himself. He was already known here and there in the north for his great strength.

But this was the perfect chance for him to show what he could really do.

"Imagine how famous I would be if I managed to kill the monster," he thought. "It would be enough to make me a great hero…and harpists would sing about my exploits for thousands of years to come."

Beowulf soon set sail for Denmark, taking with him the band of young

warriors he often led into battle. A week
or so later, he and his shield-brothers
marched through Rothgar's village, the
northern sunlight glinting on their
helmets and mailshirts, their sharp
swords and spears.

Rothgar was sitting at the far end of
his hall, deep in moody thought, his face

clouded. A few of his warriors were
standing nearby. Beowulf strode up to him,
past heaps of smashed tables and benches,

all marked with gouges and scratches. Bloodstains covered the walls, and there was no bright, warming fire burning in the dead hearth, only cold, grey ashes.

"Hail, Rothgar," said Beowulf. "I've come to solve your problem."

"Is that so?" said one of Rothgar's men, looking Beowulf up and down. The man obviously wasn't that impressed. "Well then, who are you?"

"My name is Beowulf, and these are my shield-brothers," the young warrior said, returning the man's stare. "And who might you be, friend?"

The man didn't bother to reply, but turned to Rothgar instead. "Don't listen to him, my lord," he said. "He can't help us. He's like all the others. Full of boasting, I'll bet, but no real match for a monster like Grendel."

"You're probably right, Unferth," said Rothgar. "But I think I've heard his name before. You've gained something of a reputation, Beowulf."

"True," said Beowulf, standing tall and proud before the chieftain. "So I hope that means you'll allow me to take on this evil creature for you."

"Don't ask me that..." said Rothgar.

"I would hate to see yet another young warrior slaughtered. What do you know about Grendel, anyway?"

"Not much," said Beowulf, shrugging. "Except that he haunts your hall at night, and has killed a lot of warriors. What else is there to know?"

"A great deal," said Unferth. "Grendel is strong and cunning and shows no mercy. When he chooses, he is harder to see than the shadow of a shadow. He finds ways in, where no creature of daylight could go…"

"And it also seems that no blade made by humans can harm him, nor even make a mark on his scaly hide," Rothgar muttered. "Some believe that he lives in a lake in the marshes with his mother, another creature of darkness and pure evil. So, young man – what do you say now?"

Beowulf hesitated. The truth was that he had begun to feel nervous. He hadn't fully understood just what a challenge Grendel might be till then – a straight fight was one thing, but grappling with the monster they had just described…well, that was different. But Beowulf kept an iron grip on himself, determined not to show what he was feeling inside. He hadn't come all this way only to give up at the first touch of fear.

"Exactly the same," he replied. "I'm here to rid you of this evil, and in front of every man present I swear that's what I will do. Or die trying."

Rothgar smiled, and his men seemed impressed – even Unferth.

"Very well," said Rothgar. "Tonight you will face the monster as you wish. And if you defeat him, I will reward you handsomely. But first let me feed you and your men. We still know how to treat guests here."

CHAPTER TWO

TERROR IN THE NIGHT

ROTHGAR TOLD HIS MEN TO clear up the hall as best they could, and get a fire going, and before long a marvellous feast was laid on for Beowulf and his men. Rothgar's wife came to meet

them, and laughter echoed in the rafters,
something that hadn't been heard there
for a very long time. But through the
open doorway, Beowulf could see the
daylight fading. Night was coming, and

he knew Grendel wouldn't be far behind.

Soon the feast was over, and the
moment came for Rothgar and his wife
and men to leave the hall. Rothgar wished
Beowulf luck. He gripped his hand and

talked of the gold and jewels and fine
weapons and horses he would give
him – if the young warrior survived the
night. But Beowulf could see in Rothgar's
sad eyes that the chieftain didn't think
he would...

"I won't be needing this," Beowulf
said, giving his sword to one of his
shield-brothers for
safekeeping. He
positioned them
round the hall, and
took a spot right in
the middle, by the
fire. He ordered
his men to tell
him as soon as
they heard or
saw anything,
and then he

would step forward to fight Grendel
with his bare hands. That was the plan,
at any rate.

He had done plenty of wrestling in his time, and had beaten many strong men.

They settled down to wait, the darkness in the doorway deepening. Beowulf sat by the flickering firelight, the flames shrinking, the shadows in the corners of the hall lengthening and flowing into each other. One by one, Beowulf's men fell asleep, their chins nodding onto their chests. But Beowulf stayed awake.

Then his eyelids began to grow heavy too.

All at once the monster Grendel exploded out of the darkness, hissing and spitting and slashing at Beowulf with his sharp, curved talons.

The young warrior was knocked off
his feet, crashing into the hearth
and sending a shower
of sparks flying,
although he
still managed
to hold back
the monster.
Beowulf was
on his back
now with
Grendel on
top of him, the
monster snarling
and snapping
and trying to rip
out his throat.

Grendel stank of the marshes, and was slimy to the touch. He was incredibly strong too, exactly as Unferth had said. He pressed down on Beowulf, his foul breath beating into the young warrior's face, drool dripping from his pointed, yellow fangs.

Beowulf resisted with all his might,
and slowly began to force Grendel back.
He heard his shield-brothers shouting,
and suddenly a torch flared into life,
then another.

Beowulf could see his opponent now, the
thick, scaly, grey hide, the body like a

man's, although much bigger and rippling with muscle. The young warrior rolled to one side, holding the monster's wrists and trying to get on top of him. Soon they were on their knees, then on their feet, neither of them willing to let go, the terrible struggle continuing.

Monster and man stared at each other, their faces almost touching. Beowulf's men hacked at Grendel with their swords, but he seemed not to notice. He started pressing Beowulf down once more, torchlight glinting in his black eyes. His mouth widened in a wicked smile, and those yellow fangs came closer and closer to the soft flesh of Beowulf's throat…

Beowulf summoned up all his massive strength.

He squeezed the
monster's wrists
and pushed
back at him
again – and
gradually he
began to win.
"You've met
your match at
last, Grendel."
he muttered
from between
gritted teeth,
and the monster's
smile faded. Soon Beowulf could see fear
in the monster's eyes, and feel him trying
to pull away.

Eventually Beowulf pinned Grendel down, and secured both of the monster's wrists in one mighty hand. Then with the other he reached for Grendel's throat. Strangling would probably be the best way to kill him.

Grendel squealed in panic, freed one arm and desperately tried to escape.

Beowulf held on grimly, and warrior and monster crashed round the hall, smashing into the walls and knocking over Beowulf's men like so many skittles.

At last there was a great sound of flesh tearing and bones cracking, and the monster fled, howling, into the night, leaving Beowulf holding a strange and grisly trophy – Grendel's other arm and shoulder.

Beowulf nailed it to a beam, and his men cheered him to the rafters.

CHAPTER THREE

VICTORY!

IN THE MORNING, WHEN ROTHGAR returned to his hall, he was amazed to see Grendel's arm.

Of course he was also delighted that Beowulf had lived to tell the incredible tale of what had happened. And he was even more delighted with the news that Unferth brought him soon after.

"We followed Grendel's trail all the way to the lake in the marshes, my lord," said Unferth. "That's where it stops. The monster must have been returning to his lair. And the water is stained red with his blood."

"He couldn't possibly have survived such a wound…" said Rothgar. "Which means, Beowulf, that you are the greatest hero of our time!"

The young warrior grinned as everyone cheered again. Then Rothgar laid on an even more magnificent feast, and brought out wonderful gifts for Beowulf and his men – all the fine things he had talked of, and lots more besides. Beowulf ate and drank and listened to the harpist singing, hardly able to believe that his exploits were the subject of the song.

That night, as he finally lay down to rest in Rothgar's hall along with everyone else, he felt utterly exhausted. He was bruised and battered too, and he knew that it had been a desperately close-run contest. The monster had tested him to the very limits of his strength.

Another moment or two and one of his arms might have been ripped out, not Grendel's.

"Well, thank goodness it's all over, anyway," thought Beowulf. He smiled as he remembered what Rothgar had said, and fell asleep...

But it wasn't over. He woke to the sound of screaming. People were running round in terror, their shadows dancing in the firelight.

A huge shape snarled and slashed at anyone who was near, and finally vanished.

Torches flared, and Beowulf heard gasps, followed by howls of grief.

He quickly pushed through the crowd and saw Rothgar by a pool of blood.

A trail of red footprints led from the blood to the hall door. And Grendel's arm was gone, pulled down from the wall and carried off into the night.

"Grim news, Beowulf," said Rothgar, turning to him. "Death still stalks my hall. I've lost another brave warrior to a monster from the marsh."

"What, you mean that Grendel isn't dead?" said Beowulf.

"Oh, Grendel is dead, right enough," Rothgar muttered, his face grim. "The beast who came here tonight had both her arms… I had always thought the story about Grendel having a mother was a tale to frighten little children. But it's true, and she came to seek revenge for her son."

CHAPTER FOUR

A MOTHER'S REVENGE

EVERYBODY IN THE HALL started talking at once, their fear and horror making them loud. Before long they convinced themselves that Grendel's mother was impossibly strong and far more powerful than her son, and that she would return to hunt them each night, just as he had done.

"What shall we do?" somebody wailed at last. "We're all doomed!"

"Oh no we're not!" somebody else yelled. "Beowulf will save us!"

"Yes, Beowulf!" the crowd yelled. They turned to the young warrior, and they started to chant his name. "Beowulf! BEOWULF! BEOWULF!"

"ENOUGH!" Rothgar shouted at last, and the hall fell silent. "No man should be forced to fight such a hellish creature," said Rothgar. "And if you choose not to, Beowulf, you can still leave here with the gifts I gave you, and feel no shame. You've done your share, and I thank you."

All eyes were on the young warrior now. Beowulf was silent, deep in thought, his head down. Then he looked up at Rothgar, and at Unferth.

"And what if there is another monster, after I kill this one?" he said.

"Beowulf, there is always another monster," Rothgar said. "Or armies of invaders like hungry wolves in the winter, or other threats…"

And that's when Beowulf realised there was a lot more to this business of being a hero than he had thought. It seemed it wasn't just about glory, and harpists singing songs about your exploits. These people were relying on him. They had seen him take on one monster and win,

and now they were expecting him to
defeat a bigger, stronger, scarier opponent.

But what if he couldn't do it? Beowulf
scanned the ring of faces before him, saw
the hope and trust in their eyes – the
belief that he would succeed again
and save them. Suddenly all the fear
inside him fell away. He knew
he couldn't let these people
down, even if it meant
losing his life.

"So be it,"
he said,
standing tall
and proud.
"I choose…
to fight!"

A great roar went up in the hall, and soon Beowulf and his shield-brothers were on the trail of Grendel's mother.

Her huge footprints were plain to see beside the blood trail left by Grendel.

Rothgar had promised Beowulf more fine gifts, but the only thing on Beowulf's mind was killing the monster. He didn't care any more if harpists sang about him afterwards.

They did, though. They sang of how Beowulf found a mist-covered lake in the marshes, of how he plunged deep beneath its tainted surface and tracked Grendel's mother to her cave, of how he fought a mighty fight with her over the body of her dead son – and of how he won. They sang of how he returned with the heads of both monsters, and left Rothgar and his people free forever from the terror that had haunted their nights.

And we still sing the same song today – that of Beowulf the hero!

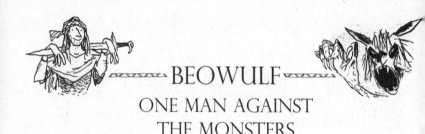

BEOWULF
ONE MAN AGAINST
THE MONSTERS

BY TONY BRADMAN

Nobody knows whether one man or many created the story of Beowulf. We don't know when it was first told – some people think that might have been in the 8th century AD, others in 1000 AD or later. And we nearly didn't have it at all – the only manuscript was almost burnt in a fire in the 16th century.

We do know that it was originally a poem in Old English, the language of the Anglo-Saxons who invaded Britain and settled here after the Romans left. We also know that some of the people in the poem actually existed – Rothgar was a real king, and archaeologists have excavated his great hall in Denmark.

Like the Vikings, who invaded Britain later on, the Anglo-Saxons were a warrior people. Their Gods were fierce and demanded the sacrifice of animals, and sometimes even human beings. The Anglo-Saxons loved to hear stories of men fighting and courage in war, and also of strange, mythical monsters.

All these things came together in the story of Beowulf. Perhaps he did exist, and did travel to help Rothgar. And perhaps a tale of his adventures was passed from person to person, then made into a poem to be told on winter evenings in the hall of a great lord, his people feasting around him, the hearth fire flickering.

It's not surprising that a magical thread was woven into the story – what is more natural in the tale of a legendary hero than an encounter with a mythical monster? Beowulf's battle with Grendel is a lot like the tales of Greek heroes such as Theseus and the Minotaur, and Perseus killing the Gorgon, Medusa.

But there was something about the character of Beowulf that has made people want to read his story over and over again, or make it into longer stories and even films. That something is the way in which Beowulf shows true courage. He kills one monster – but then he has to fight a far worse one, Grendel's mother. Beowulf shows us that one person can face many problems – and survive.

THE GREATEST ADVENTURES IN THE WORLD

TONY BRADMAN & TONY ROSS